Iktomi Loses His Eyes

Hi kids!
I'M IKTOMI!!
This is more lies about me by that white guy, Paul Goble.
He says I've lost my eyes and can't see proper.
I've warned you about him before.
And he doesn't give me a penny of his royalties.
So tell your librarians to ban the book.
Huh?
You're cool kids!
I luv yer!

Iktomi's other misadventures:

Iktomi and the Boulder
Iktomi and the Berries
Iktomi and the Ducks
Iktomi and the Buffalo Skull
Iktomi and the Buzzard
Iktomi and the Coyote

and the books not about Iktomi:

Crow Chief
Remaking the Earth

also:

Custer's Last Battle
The Fetterman Fight
Lone Bull's Horse Raid
The Friendly Wolf
The Girl Who Loved Wild Horses
The Gift of the Sacred Dog
Buffalo Woman
The Great Race
Star Boy
Death of the Iron Horse
Her Seven Brothers
Beyond the Ridge
Dream Wolf
I Sing for the Animals
Love Flute
The Lost Children
Adopted by the Eagles
The Return of the Buffaloes
The Legend of the White Buffalo Woman

Hau Kola—Hello Friend
(an autobiography for children)

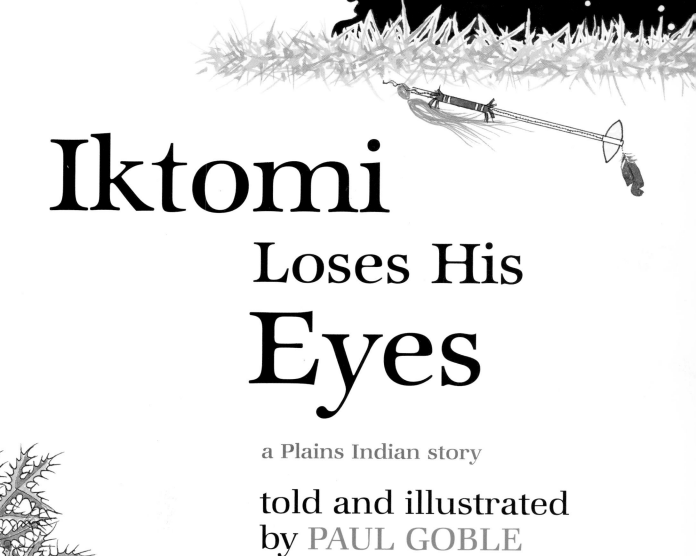

Iktomi Loses His Eyes

a Plains Indian story

told and illustrated
by PAUL GOBLE

Orchard Books New York

This book is for
Iktomi's friends—
this means you.

DeRe WiFe
ive Gon GaMBuLLinG
ive BoRoWeD The GRoaceRy Money
IKTo

References

Deloria, Ella, *Dakota Texts*, Publications of the American Ethnological Society, Vol. 14, New York, 1932. Dorsey, George and Alfred L. Kroeber, *Traditions of the Arapaho*, Field Museum of Natural History, Anthropological Series V, Chicago, 1903. Erdoes, Richard, *The Sound of Flutes*, Pantheon Books, New York, 1976. Grinnell, George Bird, *By Cheyenne Campfires*, Yale University Press, New Haven, 1926; *Blackfoot Lodge Tales*, Charles Scribner's Sons, New York, 1892. Kroeber, Alfred L., *Cheyenne Tales, The Journal of American Folk-Lore*, Vol. XIII, New York, 1900. Law, Kathryn, *Tales from the Bitterroot Valley and Other Salish Folk Tales*, Montana Reading Publications, Billings, 1971. Linderman, Frank B., *Indian Old-Man Stories*, Charles Scribner's Sons, New York, 1920. Rides at the Door, Darnell Davis, *Napi Stories*, Blackfeet Heritage Program, Browning, 1979. Stands in Timber, John and Margo Liberty, *Cheyenne Memories*, Yale University Press, New Haven, 1967. Tall Bull, Henry and Tom Weist, *Ve'ho*, Montana Reading Publications, Billings, 1971. Thompson, Stith, *Tales of the North American Indians*, Indiana University Press, Bloomington, 1926. Wissler, Clark and D. C. Duvall, *Mythology of the Blackfoot Indians*, Anthropological Papers of the American Museum of Natural History, Vol. 2, Part 1, New York, 1908.

 Orchard Books, A Grolier Company, 95 Madison Avenue, New York, NY 10016. Manufactured in the United States of America. Printed and bound by Phoenix Color Corp. The text of this book is set in 22 point ITC Zapf Book Light. Library of Congress Cataloging-in-Publication Data. Goble, Paul. Iktomi loses his eyes : a Plains Indian story / by Paul Goble. p. cm. Summary: Iktomi the trickster finds himself in a predicament after losing his eyes when he misuses a magical trick. ISBN 0-531-30200-8 (trade : alk. paper)—ISBN 0-531-33200-4 (lib. bdg. : alk. paper) 1. Iktomi (Legendary character)—Legends. 2. Indians of North America—Great Plains—Folklore. 3. Legends—Great Plains. [1. Iktomi (Legendary character)—Legends. 2. Indians of North America—Great Plains—Folklore. 3. Folklore—Great Plains.] I. Title. E78.G73G62 1999 398.2'089'97—dc21 99-12036

The illustrations are India ink and watercolor on Oram & Robinson [England] Limited Watercolor Board, reproduced in combined line and halftone. Book design by Paul Goble. 10 9 8 7 6 5 4 3 2 1

About Iktomi

The Lakota Trickster is called Iktomi, which means "spider." In these stories, he is a reflection of our baser selves, with his spiderlike cleverness, untrustworthiness, and stupidity. Here he is once again, running after the latest bit of fashionable nonsense. This time it is an eye-juggling trick, but in taking it to excess, he loses his sight. Don't we all lose our focus and sense of proportion over the latest fads? To get his sight back, Iktomi takes unfair advantage of the innocence and kindness of Mouse and Buffalo and borrows an eye from each. This does not fully restore his sight, for he can see only what is far away and what is at the end of his nose, but nothing immediately around him, which, again, reflects our own predicament.

North American Trickster stories, like all traditional stories, speak on different levels, cloaking deeper meanings that teach or provoke philosophical discussion. Today the stories are thought of as just whimsical tales to entertain children, but in the old days, they were stories for young and old. A person's faults and idiosyncrasies were likened to Iktomi. People gathered to listen and tell these stories, and each story might end with the question, "And who will tie one to that?" Someone would answer, "I will," and so the storytelling would continue.

A tipi village, usually quite small in numbers of people, was a closely knit community. It had to be well ordered and with high moral standards for people to live harmoniously. Possibly the stories about Iktomi's wickedness were small safety valves, to give expression to thoughts that were otherwise considered antisocial or taboo, a reminder *not* to be like Iktomi. The morals were implied, but not spelled out as in Aesop's fables.

You cannot get close to Iktomi with a scientific mind. He is like all of us, more complex than we can ever figure out, making nonsense of rules and labels and psychoanalysis. We should just enjoy him for who he is—for all his stupidity, pomposity, greed, vanity, laziness, wickedness, and any other negative qualities you may wish to add!

A Note for the Reader

There is no "authentic" version of these stories. The only rule in telling them is to include certain basic themes. They were told with the expectation that listeners would interject their own comments. The opportunity for this is given where the text changes to gray type. At this time, Iktomi's thoughts, printed in small type, might also be included. They are not meant to be read aloud, because they would break the flow of the story.

Iktomi has no respect for language. Among his many human failings, he is lazy, and he never bothers "to speak proper."

Why is that guy waving at me?

Iktomi was walking along. . . .

Don't all Iktomi stories start out this way?

Iktomi was walking along.
"I get so tired of people," he was thinking. "I've had enough of everyone putting me down, telling me what to do."

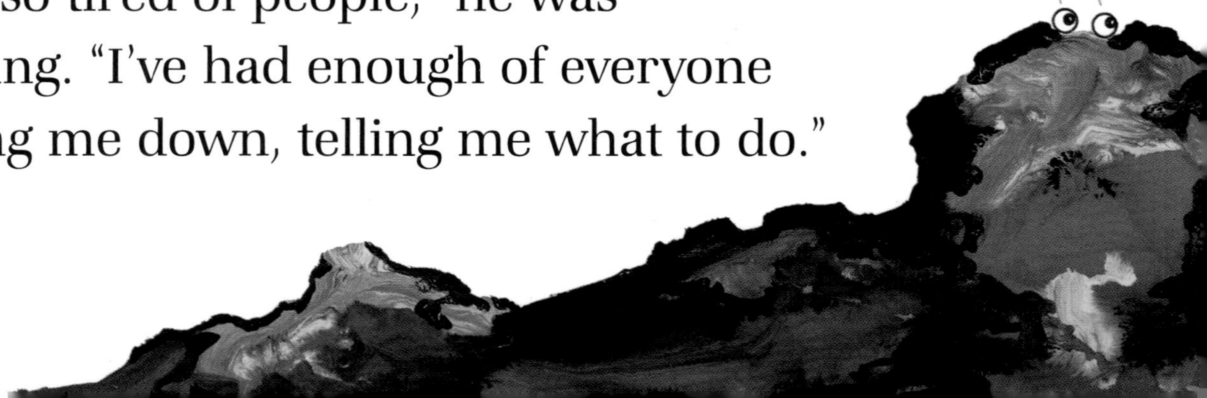

My eagle feathers
My roach
Today I'm getting in touch
with my subconscious.
My face paint
I am happy being Iktomi!
My ribbon-shirt
My porcupine-quillwork
breastplate
My pipe and tobacco bag
My blanket
My trade-cloth leggings
My moccasins

"I don't like *anyone. Nobody* likes me."

Do you sometimes feel like that?

"So on this fine day I'm getting in touch with my heritage. I've painted my face, and I'm wearing my traditional clothes. I step into my ancestors' moccasins, and I feel proud and worthwhile."

Boy! I really look
better than I thought.

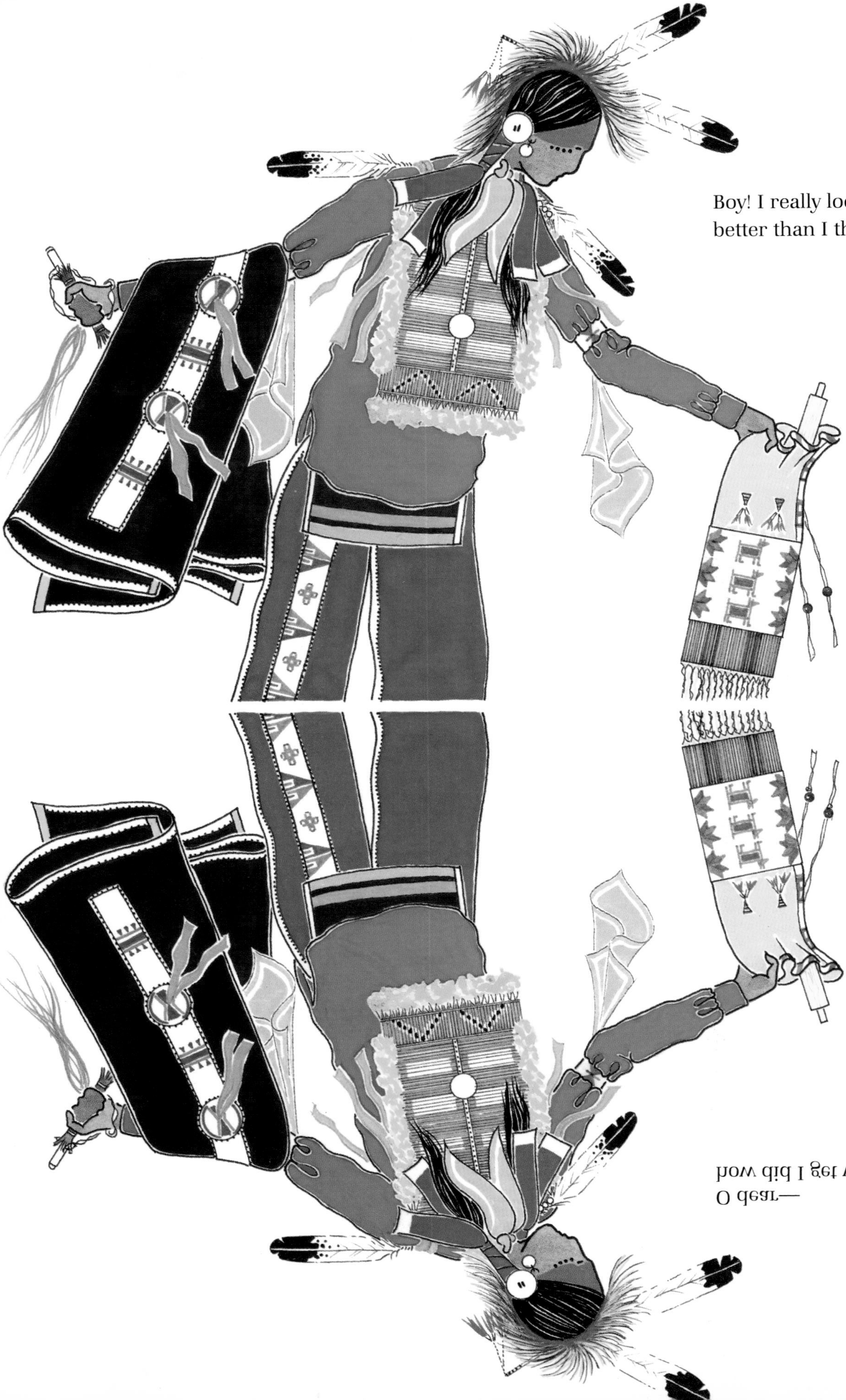

O dear—
how did I get wet feet?

"Ah! Let me look at myself. This puddle will be my mirror. No . . . there's *nobody* better looking than Iktomi."

Yes, and we all know Iktomi is a great show-off, don't we?

"I like myself. Yes, I really do.
And . . . today I'm carrying my great-great-great-great-grandfather's stone-headed tomahawk.
I'll crack anyone over the head who tries to use me as a doormat!"

Iktomi is in a warlike mood, isn't he?

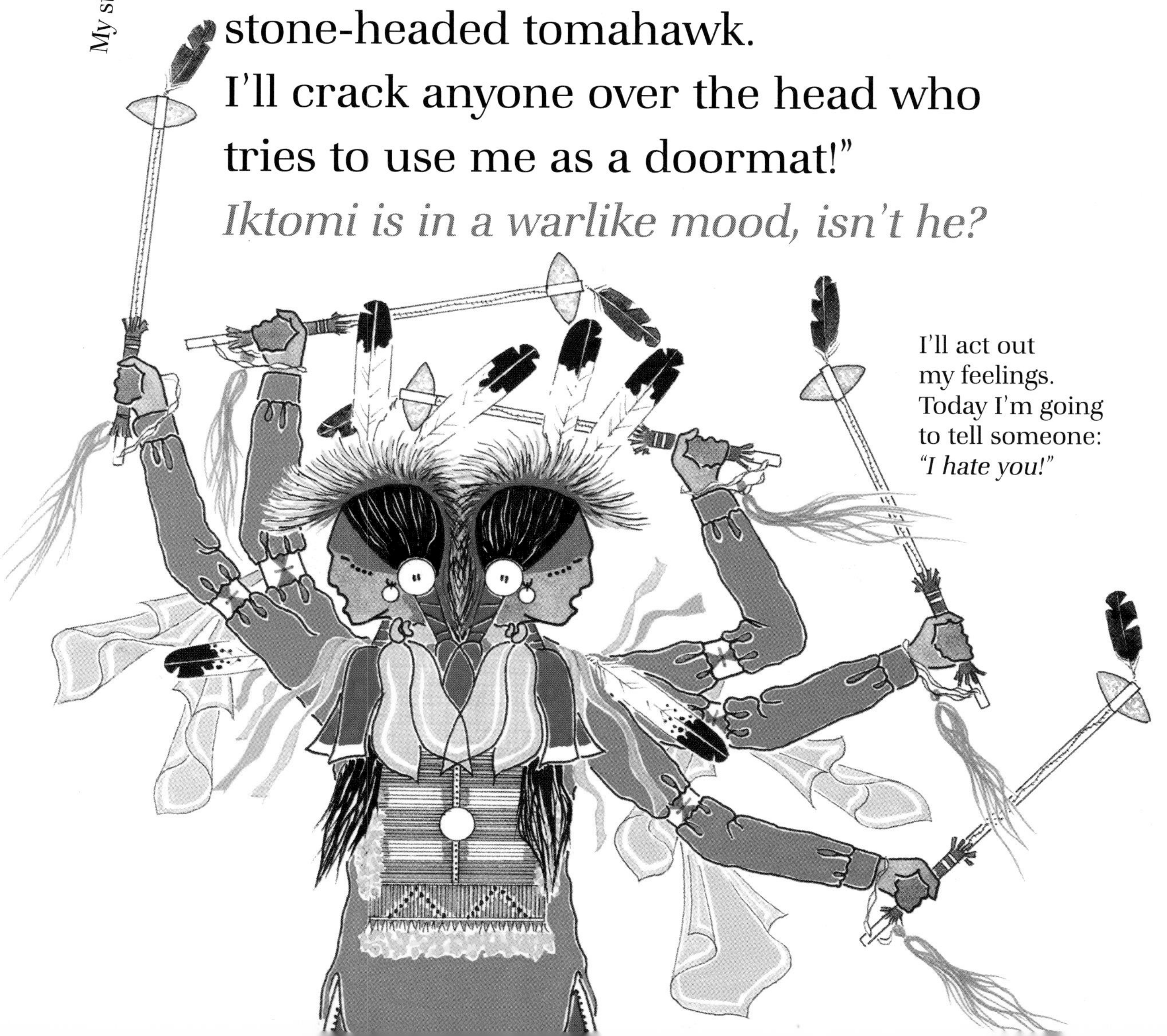
My stone-headed tomahawk!
I'll act out my feelings. Today I'm going to tell someone: *"I hate you!"*

Just then Iktomi caught sight of a man in the distance who was acting strangely and talking to himself. Iktomi crept cautiously forward and hid behind a bush to see what was going on.

Does he really imagine he cannot be seen behind that bush?

I can't live a moment longer
without being able to do that.

The man
was saying,
"Eyes, fly from
my head to the
top of that post! *Go!*"
And his eyes left his head
and flew through the air to
the top of a fence post.
"Eyes, *come back!*" he called,
and his eyes flew back into his
head.

Iktomi was in awe. . . .
He had never, ever, seen
such a clever trick.

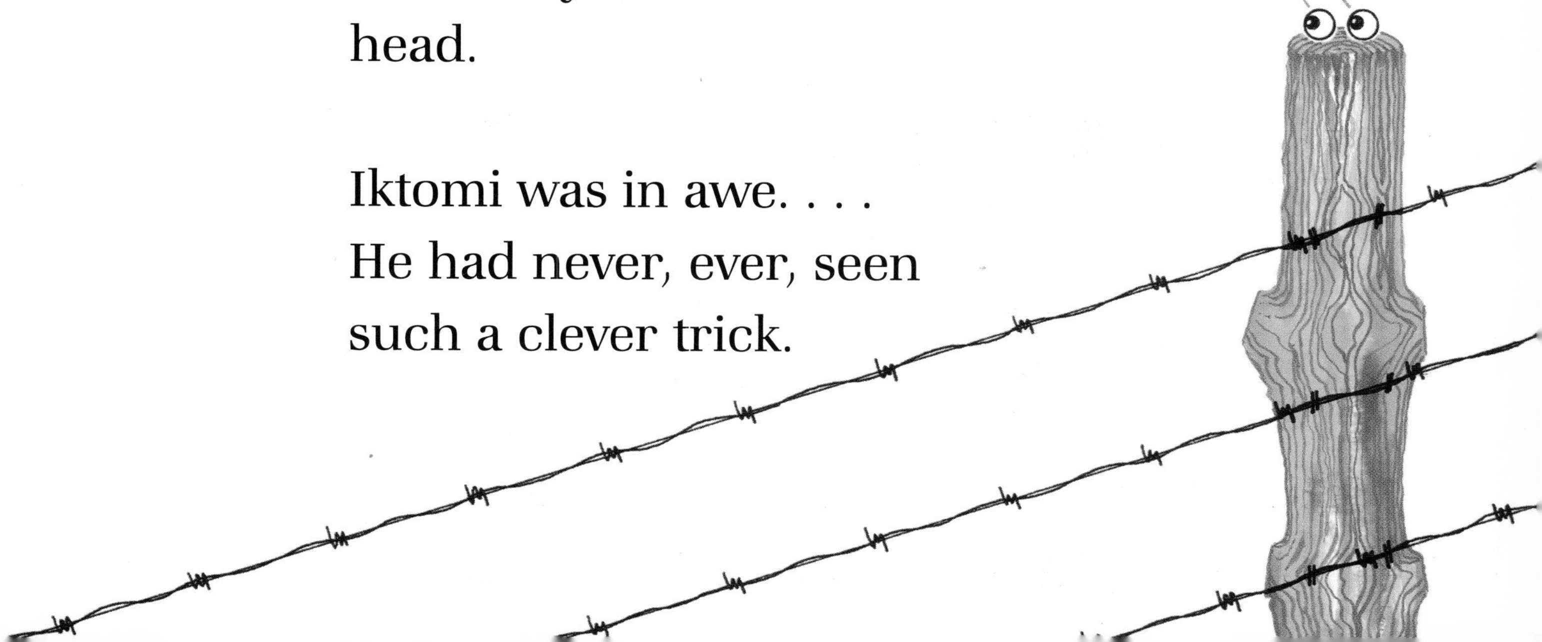

Iktomi ran up to the man and said, "Brother, how do you do that *wonderful* trick? I want to do it too! Please teach me! *Please!*" And he began to cry. *"P-l-e-a-s-e!"*

"Okay, don't upset yourself," the man answered. "But I tell you, don't do the trick more than four times a day. If you do it more than four times, something bad will happen. Here, sign your name on this paper."

When Iktomi had signed his name, the man told him, "Now you can do it. *Remember, not more than four times a day,"* he repeated, *"or something bad will happen."*

I *want* to do that!
I *need* to do that!
If I could do that trick, everyone
would think I was the cleverest person
in
the
whole
world.

LAND SALE
Iktomi
Hed Cheaf.

Do you think Ikto is listening?

Third go!!!
I've still got one more to go.
Second go!!

"Eyes," Iktomi said, "fly from my head to the top of that white cloud. *Go!*" His eyes left his head and flew through the air to the cloud. "Eyes, *come back!*" he called, and his eyes came back into his head and he could see again. "This is *great*! I can't wait to show everyone! That time didn't count; I was just experimenting."

???

Iktomi went on his way, happy with his new trick. He soon did it again. "That's once," he told himself.

But he has done it twice, hasn't he?

He did it a third and a fourth time. "That makes three times," he said.

He has really done it four times. . . .

First go!
Just practicing—
that time didn't count.

Soon Iktomi met some of his friends.
"Brothers and sisters, I am *so* glad to have found you. I want to show you my new power. Watch!
Eyes, fly to the top of that tree! *Go!*"
And his eyes flew to the very top.
Everyone was amazed.

What do you think will happen now?

"Eyes, *come back!*" Iktomi called.
But, they did not. . . .
"Eyes, *come back! Now!*" he shouted.
"EYES, COME BACK!!!
Oh help . . . I can't see. . . ."
He knew he had cheated on counting.
His friends walked away.
"Silly Ikto," they laughed.

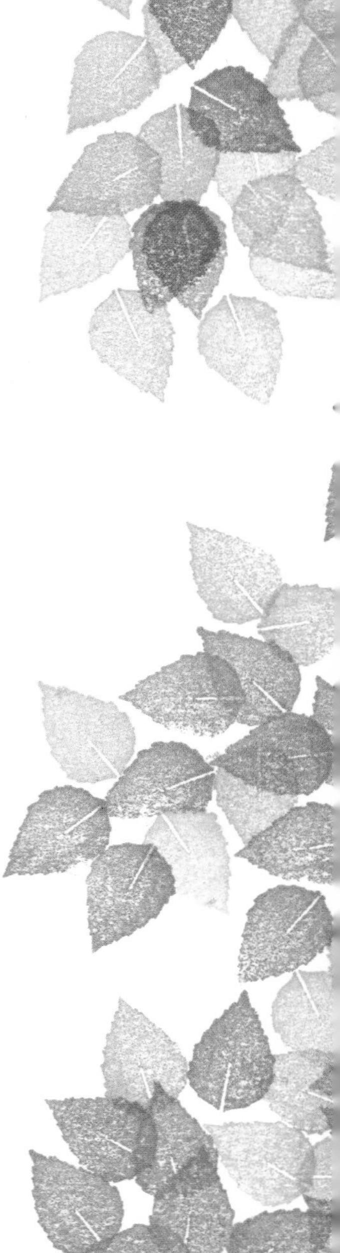

Oh, how embarrassing. . . .
But even so . . . did it
impress them just a little?

. . . and now?

Who
got
me
into
this
mess?

Squirrel, who was climbing in the tree,
came upon Iktomi's eyes.
"Chat! Chatt! Chattt! Chatttt!
These look like Iktomi's eyes.
He'll want them back one day.
I'll store them in Woodpecker's old
nest hole."

Iktomi heard Squirrel talking.
"Little Brother, give me my eyes."
But Squirrel was chattering, climbing
here and there, and did not hear.
You have heard Squirrel chattering.

Iktomi could not see anything.
He felt around for the tree,
and climbed up among the branches.
He could not find Woodpecker's nest
hole. A branch broke and he fell . . .

. . . and landed on his back,
altogether tangled up
in a thicket of thornbushes.

Ouch!!!
......!
......!
......!

He untangled himself and walked on, slowly, arms outstretched, so as not to bump into anything, but he tripped over rocks and fell again.
He gave up.
He just lay there,
and cried and cried.
Ohhhhhhh . . .

As he lay there, he felt a little tongue licking his tears.

"Who are you?" Iktomi asked.

"It's me, Mouse. What makes you so sad on this lovely day, older brother?"

"Oh, my little brother," Iktomi replied, "I forgot to bring my eyes and now I cannot find my way home to my wife."

What do you think of that story?

"Little brother, please be very kind: lend me your eyes."

"How could I then find *my* way home?" Mouse asked. "But you can have *one* eye. I hope it will help you get back home again."

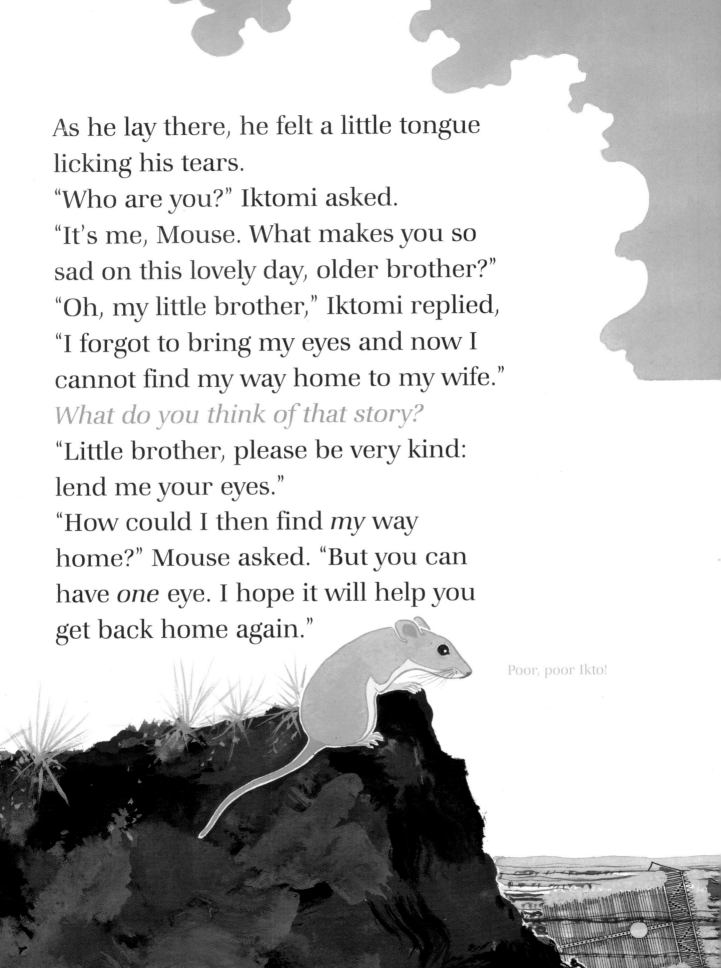

Poor, poor Ikto!

Iktomi then had a single tiny eye. He could see what was very close, but it did not stop him from falling into a river. . . .

He's nice, for a mouse.
But I still can't see proper.

Iktomi pulled himself out onto the bank. He just lay there and cried.

He cries a lot, doesn't he?

Buffalo came from far off and across the prairie to find out why he was crying.

"I cannot see," sobbed Iktomi.

"I lent my eyes to my best friend, but he never gave them back."

Hmmmmmm?

"I cannot find my way home, and my wife will be crying for me."

Do you think so?

"Oh, younger brother, please be kind: lend me one of your eyes?"

Buffalo gave Iktomi one of his eyes.

"Take it, older brother," Buffalo said.

"One eye is enough for me, so long as you can see."

What
a sad
story. . . .

Buffalo's only an animal:
big eye—small brain.

How do I look, kids?
Pretty good? Huh?

And so Iktomi had one enormous eye bulging out of his head, and the other eye no larger than the smallest black bead. He could see what was far away, and he could see what was close up against his nose, but nothing in between.

He could *not* find his way home.

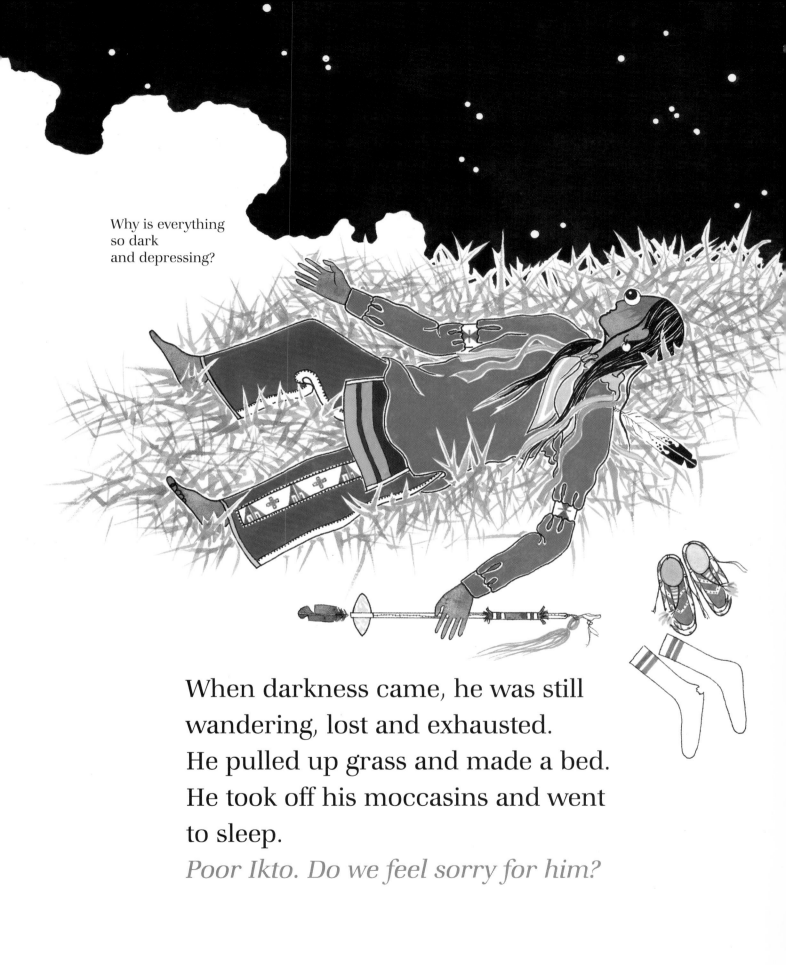

Why is everything
so dark
and depressing?

When darkness came, he was still wandering, lost and exhausted. He pulled up grass and made a bed. He took off his moccasins and went to sleep.

Poor Ikto. Do we feel sorry for him?

Eagle

Iktomi did not know why he awoke in the night, but when he opened his eyes, what he thought he saw in the moonlight made his hair

stand on end with terror!!!

At the foot of his grass bed, ghostly hands were waving, side to side . . . slowly waving, side to side. . . .

Very stealthily he reached for his great-great-great-great-grandfather's tomahawk.

Gripping it firmly, he swung it with all his might at the ghostly hands—

WHAM!

"OUCH!!! HELP!!! Oh . . . help!"

What he thought were ghostly hands were really his own feet!

What do you think about that?!

Iktomi hopped around like a grasshopper in a prairie fire.

When the sun came up, he finally found his way home. His appearance gave his wife a terrible fright. "W-Whatever—*whatever* have you been up to now, you silly old man? Don't come back here looking like *that*! Go and find your things, *and put some shoes on!*" she scolded.

"Even my wife . . . ," pondered Iktomi. "I dislike *everyone*. *Nobody* likes me."

Don't blame me!
It was the other guy who done it!
Mrs. Iktomi

And after that what should I do?

Iktomi went on his way,
limping on tender, hurting feet,
and muttering to himself,
"I'll find Squirrel and ask him to give
me back my eyes."

*Do you think Ikto will ever see again?
And can anyone guess what he will be
up to after that?*